For Lori Kilkelly —S.M.

*For Mary Viruleg, my math teacher who made
me believe I could be an engineer —D.S.*

Library of Congress Cataloging-in-Publication Data
Names: McAnulty, Stacy, author. | Marlin, Lissy, illustrator.
Title: Goldie Blox rules the school! / by Stacy McAnulty ;
[illustrated by Lissy Marlin].
Description: First edition. | New York : Random House, 2017. | Series:
Goldie Blox and the Gearheads ; book 1
Identifiers: LCCN 2016025778 | ISBN 978-0-399-55634-0 (paperback) |
ISBN 978-0-399-55635-7 (lib. bdg.) | ISBN 978-0-399-55648-7 (ebook)
Subjects: | BISAC: JUVENILE FICTION / Media Tie-In. | JUVENILE FICTION /
Humorous Stories. | JUVENILE FICTION / Science & Technology.
Classification: LCC PZ7.M47825255 Gol 2017 | DDC [Fic]—dc23

Visit us on the Web!
randomhousekids.com
goldieblox.com
Printed in the United States of America
10 9 8 7 6 5 4 3 2 1

This book has been officially leveled by using the
F&P Text Level Gradient™ Leveling System.

Random House Children's Books supports the
First Amendment and celebrates the right to read.

Goldie 🦍 *Blox*®

GOLDIE BLOX ~~RUINS~~ RULES THE SCHOOL!

Written by Stacy McAnulty
Illustrated by Lissy Marlin

Random House 🏠 New York

OFFICIALLY CLOSED

The first alarm clock rang. Goldie Blox snored on. The second alarm buzzed. Goldie didn't lift an eyelid. The third alarm clock blared like a siren, and her bed's ejection mechanism threw her across the room.

She landed at the top of a slide. Two whirling mechanical arms pulled a T-shirt over her head and gave her a push. Goldie slid down into a pair of overalls. At the bottom of the slide, a spring shot her to the ceiling fan. She twirled around and around until her crazy hair was even crazier—exactly how she liked it. Then she let go and sailed off the fan and onto a trampoline. As she bounced, four toothbrushes cleaned her teeth before she jumped off and went flying again. She landed upside down in her laundry basket.

"I'm awake. I'm awake!"

Nacho, her basset hound, pulled her out of the basket. He licked her cheek.

"I was supposed to land in my sneakers. And not upside down. I'll make some adjustments for tomorrow." Goldie scratched her pet under his chin. She tilted her nose up into the air. "Do you smell that?"

Nacho sniffed his pawpits. If something smelled bad, it was usually coming from him.

"It's Dad's famous cornflake, peanut butter, and bacon waffles! He only makes them on special occasions." Goldie yanked on her

sneakers. "Let's go, Nacho."

She twirled down the fireman's pole into the kitchen. It was two seconds faster than taking the twisty slide. Nacho jumped into a motorized shopping cart and rode the tracks right to his food bowl.

Junie and Beau Blox, Goldie's parents, sat quietly at the table. Goldie could tell right away that this was not a celebration.

"Mom, Dad, what's up? You didn't go into the BloxShop, did you?" Goldie had left a bit of a mess—more like a disaster—in her workshop. Her food converter was still in the prototype stage. Instead of turning an orange into a lollipop, it had blown the orange to smithereens. Then it had blown up an apple, a watermelon, and two pineapples. The BloxShop looked like the inside of a blender.

"What did you do, Goldie?" her mom asked.

She shook her head. "Never mind. That's not important. Sit down, sweetie."

Sweetie? This is serious, Goldie thought. She sank into a kitchen chair and took a deep breath.

"The Blox School is officially closed," her mom said. "I'm sorry."

"What? Why?" Goldie had been attending the Blox School since kindergarten. It wasn't a big, normal school. Her mom was the only teacher, and each year there were just four or five students, including Goldie. The other kids were usually new to town and didn't stay long.

"Mayor Zander shut it down," her dad said. "After you blew off the second story, the mayor was worried—"

"I didn't blow it off," Goldie interrupted. "I accidentally sent the upstairs into orbit. It'll land on Mars next year." She'd only meant to shoot a small rocket into space, not the entire second story of the school. She wished she'd double-checked her calculations. Still, the launch had been epic. It even made the nightly news.

"We know you'd never destroy something on purpose," her dad said.

"I'm sorry." Goldie brightened. "But I bet we could fix it together." Her dad worked for a construction company. It wouldn't be the first time he had helped Goldie repair something.

"That's not the plan," her mom said.

"So . . . am I not going to school anymore?" The idea wasn't awful. Goldie liked school, but without it, she'd have more time for engineering gadgets.

"Of course you're going to school," her mom said. "You'll be attending Higgs Bozon Prep." HiBo only accepted *gifted* students.

Kids who got into HiBo had to pass a series of long and difficult tests.

"Here, have some waffles," her dad said. "I added a dash of hot pepper to make them more exciting."

Goldie loaded her plate and covered the waffles with butter and syrup. "I'm not HiBo material," she said through a mouthful of waffle. "I'm not a *genius* genius."

Goldie didn't know her exact IQ. She could never sit long enough to finish the test. She was happy being a *creative* genius. Someone who would one day change the world—or accidentally cover it in maple syrup.

"Remember, I went to Higgs Bozon," her mom said. "And I've made a few calls to the school. You are officially looking at their new biology teacher. How's that for timing?" Her mom finished a cup of coffee and poured another.

"I'm not surprised." Goldie swallowed a huge bite of waffle. "You're an awesome teacher, Mom." A piece of waffle stuck in her throat as she thought of something. "Don't I have to take the tests to get into HiBo?" She shuddered.

"Since I teach there now, you're allowed to go to Higgs Bozon without taking the qualification exams," her mom told her.

"And don't forget the best part," her dad said. "You get to go to school with Li."

Li Zhang was Goldie's BFFND—best friend from next door. They'd met when they were both in diapers. Goldie was still trying to invent something to erase *that* memory.

"It's going to be great," her mom said.

Goldie wanted to believe her. But it was hard to imagine that any school could be better than the Blox School.

"When do we start?" Goldie asked.

"The first bell rings in forty-five minutes," her dad replied. "And if you have a hard time, just remember my motto. When life closes a door, what do we do?"

"Blast a hole in the roof!" Goldie yelled.

Her dad laughed. "I was going to say open a window. But that works, too." He gave her a hug. "Please don't blast a hole in anything on your first day."

AN ALUMINUM CUBE
IS FULL OF POTENTIAL

After breakfast, Goldie climbed the rope ladder up to her room. She filled a backpack with all her school supplies: her hammer, a tape measure, two screwdrivers, her graph-paper notebook that only had three unused pages, duct tape, and a can opener that was also a metal detector.

"Wish me luck," she said to Nacho, giving him a kiss goodbye.

With her skateboard tucked under one arm, she stepped onto the window ledge and grabbed the zip line that connected her house to Li's.

"Three . . . two . . . one . . . Wheeee!" Goldie sailed over the yard and landed on Li's front porch. She rang the doorbell and waited two entire seconds before letting herself in.

"Hi, Mr. Zhang!" she shouted to Li's grandfather. She had to yell to be heard over all the tick-tock noise. The house was full of hundreds of clocks, all handmade by Mr. Zhang.

"Hello, Goldie. Would you care for some prune juice?" Mr. Zhang shuffled along the hall. He only got halfway before Li flew down the stairs and landed in front of Goldie.

"Hey, G, what's up?" Li asked.

"Big news," Goldie said. "I'm going to HiBo Prep with you."

"Excellent!" Li pulled on his cap.

They said goodbye to Mr. Zhang and headed out the door. Li grabbed his hoverboard, and Goldie jumped on her skateboard.

"Race you!" Goldie took off like a bolt of lightning.

"You're on!" Li yelled from behind.

Goldie nearly fell rounding the first corner. Li was right on her tail. She weaved so that he couldn't pass.

"Eat my dust!" Goldie laughed.

"Can't," Li shouted back. "I'm taking a shortcut!" He turned down an alley and zoomed out of sight.

Goldie flipped a switch with her foot, and the skateboard's jetpacks sparked to life.

"Whoa!" Goldie shot past a bike and a motorcycle. A few seconds later, the school was in sight but Li wasn't.

Nice shortcut, Goldie thought.

Suddenly, someone knocked her off her board. Goldie rolled across the grass, colliding with knees and elbows.

"Hey!" she yelled when she stopped spinning.

"Sorry." Li groaned as he got to his feet. "Boards aren't allowed on school property. I was trying to save you from getting in trouble before you even got to your first class."

"Thanks. I think." Goldie plucked one blade

of grass from her hair, leaving a dozen more behind.

Li hid the boards behind a mailbox. Then he motioned for Goldie to follow him into HiBo Prep. It looked nothing like the Blox School. Everything from the floor to the lockers to the walls was white, black, or gray. A large aluminum cube sat in the middle of the front hall.

Goldie read the sign in front of it.

HIGGS BOZON PREP'S MASCOT. BECAUSE LIKE A STUDENT, AN ALUMINUM CUBE IS FULL OF POTENTIAL.

She slid her hands over the cube.

"What are you doing?" Li asked. "Don't touch it."

"I'm looking for the secret button." Goldie examined it from every side. "It must do something, like turn into a disco ball or a fog machine or a toaster oven. Don't kids at HiBo like toast?"

Li sighed. "It's just a cube, G."

For now, Goldie thought. She'd draw ideas in her notebook later.

In the main office, Goldie got her schedule. Li looked it over.

"Bummer, we don't have any classes together. But I'll see you at lunch." He walked her to her first class. It wasn't anywhere near her mom's new classroom. They might as well have been in different schools.

"Don't worry, G," Li said. "You'll be fine. Just don't be too creative. At least not on your first day." He gave her a fist bump. "See ya."

No sweat, Goldie thought as she took a deep breath and walked toward the classroom door. She also walked into a frowning boy with thick dark hair and square-framed glasses.

He glared at her.

"Sorry," she said. "Didn't see you."

"You new?" he asked.

"First day. My name's Goldie Blox."

The boy's eyebrows shot up. He recognized her name. Bloxtown was named after Goldie's grandmother, after all. "I'm Zeek Zander," he said.

Goldie recognized his name, too. "Are you related to Mayor Zander?"

"He's my dad," Zeek said proudly.

A small, shiny object floated behind Zeek. Goldie couldn't believe she hadn't noticed it right away.

"Is that a phone?" she asked.

"Not *just* a phone. It's a Butler Phone." Zeek smiled wickedly. "It's part phone, part hovercraft. And it can do anything." He clapped his hands twice and yelled, "Butler! Send a message to my parents that I want cookies after school."

"Done, Master Zeek. Anything else, sir?" The phone spoke with a British accent.

"Tell me what the weather will be today in Norway."

"Cloudy but mild, Master Zeek. Would you like me to book you a plane ticket?"

"Nah."

"That's so cool," Goldie said. "Did you invent it?"

Zeek's face wrinkled in confusion. "No. I ordered it online."

"Can I try?" Goldie asked.

"No way. You don't know—"

But Goldie had already made up her mind. "Butler, play some rock music. And play it like you mean it."

"Yes, miss." The sounds of an electric guitar and drums blasted through the hall. Goldie's head bobbed to the beat.

"Noooo!" Zeek yelled. "Butler, you don't take orders from her."

The music stopped at once.

"My apologies, Master Zeek," the phone said, and it floated back a few feet.

Zeek leaned over Goldie. "Never talk to my Butler Phone again."

Goldie folded her arms. "I can't. *Never* is not in my vocabulary."

As Zeek and Goldie scowled at each other, the first bell rang. Or maybe Goldie was hearing a ringing in her ears from the loud music. She followed Zeek into the classroom and found an empty seat in the back row.

ROBOT TUG-OF-WAR

After a few announcements, their teacher Mr. Greg began class with a quiz.

"I'm an A-plus teacher, so I expect A-plus grades," he said from his desk. Mr. Greg didn't get up to hand out papers. Instead, a sleek robot rolled forward from the shadows. Across its chest was written TEACHATRON 5000. It zoomed through the class, and every student had a quiz within seconds.

Wow, Goldie thought. *I'd love to take that apart and see how it works.*

"You may begin the quiz," Mr. Greg said.

Since it was her first day, Goldie knew she might be behind. Still, she wanted to give it her best shot. She dug through her backpack looking for a pen or pencil.

I must have one in here somewhere, she thought.

No pen. No pencil. Then she remembered. She ran a hand through her crazy hair and pulled out a purple marker. It wasn't just a marker. It was also a hole punch and a toothbrush. Goldie liked every tool to have more than one function.

She read the first question on the test. *I know this!* She was about to write down the correct answer when Mr. Greg yelled from the front of the room, "What is that, Miss Blox?"

Everyone looked up.

Goldie froze, her hand inches from the test.

"A marker."

"A marker? We only use click-o-matic pencils in this class. It's rule number seventeen." Mr. Greg pointed to a list on the wall.

Goldie squinted to read it. "Wowzies! This class has one hundred twenty-three rules." She couldn't believe it. It would take her a year to come up with that many rules.

"Remove that marker," Mr. Greg ordered the Teachatron 5000.

The sleek robot rolled over to Goldie's desk. The pinchy claws latched onto the marker. But Goldie refused to let go. Suddenly, she was in a tug-of-war with a robot. Unfortunately for the Teachatron, Goldie did not like to lose. She yanked as hard as she could.

"Yes!" Goldie held the marker over her head. The robot's arm was still attached to it.

"Oh no!" Mr. Greg shrieked. "My darling." He hugged the broken Teachatron and sobbed.

"Whoopsie." Goldie tried to hand Mr. Greg the robot arm. "I'm sorry."

Mr. Greg kept crying. "No, no, no."

"Hey, Zeek," Goldie whispered. "Can I borrow a clicky pencil?" He had three sitting on his desk.

"No. You need to come prepared." Zeek refused to look at her.

"I can't go on!" Mr. Greg wailed. "Class is over." He wheeled his Teachatron out of the room. The students stared, shocked.

"You've ruined everything," Zeek growled. "Who doesn't bring a pencil to school?"

A girl in a gray hoodie and pink glasses turned around in her seat. Goldie worried she might yell at her, too. But instead, the girl handed Goldie a new click-o-matic pencil.

"Thanks, I'm—" The girl turned back around before Goldie could introduce herself.

"What do we do now without Mr. Greg and the Teachatron?" someone in the front row asked.

The students all shrugged.

"We could dissect the Teachatron's arm," Goldie suggested.

Twenty kids stared at her with their mouths wide open.

"If we know how it works, it'll be easy to reattach when Mr. Greg comes back." No one agreed with her. But no one disagreed either. Goldie took the robot arm to the front of the room. She used her screwdrivers to take it apart. The entire class watched but said nothing as she removed wires and mini motors. Goldie was still fiddling with the arm when the bell rang and the class filed silently out of the room.

Things will get better, Goldie thought.

But they didn't.

In the next class, when Goldie got up to use the bathroom, the teacher practically fainted. "We do not get out of our seats without permission," he said.

Goldie didn't have the right uniform for

gym class. And in programming class, she suggested they create software that could turn frowns into smiles in pictures. The entire class laughed, but Goldie hadn't been joking.

By last period, Goldie was tired and frustrated and embarrassed. Her first day at HiBo Prep had been a dud.

SLIM, ITCHY FARTS

That night, Goldie helped her dad make dinner. He used the blowtorch to cook the chicken. She worked the table saw to slice the bread. Nacho, who wore safety goggles like Goldie and her dad, took care of the crumbs.

Her mom walked in as they were setting the table. Her hair and clothes were a mess. "Whew! Higgs Bozon is *not* a school for slackers!" She looked exhausted. "How was your day?" she asked Goldie.

Goldie shrugged. "Fine."

Her dad stared at her, and his eyebrows knitted together. He obviously didn't believe things were fine. Not now, and not when he'd asked her earlier.

"How was your day, Junie?" He kissed his wife's cheek.

"Tiring." Goldie's mom fell into a kitchen chair.

Goldie's dad scooped potatoes onto a plate with a small garden shovel and set it down in front of Goldie's mom.

"Goldie, tell us about your day," her mom said.

"Well . . ." Goldie thought about everything that went wrong. "I think I like the Blox School better."

Her dad put a comforting hand on her arm. "We didn't do a good job preparing you for a school like Higgs Bozon Prep."

"That's for sure," Goldie said.

"But you're smart and creative," her dad said.

"And hardworking," her mom added.

"We will help you any way we can," her dad said. "So what can we do?"

Goldie smiled. "Can we go pencil shopping?"

Goldie was a quick learner. The next day, she took the shortcut to school with Li. She hid her skateboard without needing to be tackled. She asked permission to go to the bathroom. In Mr. Greg's class, she didn't get into a fight with the one-armed Teachatron, and she had the right pencil. Of course, she'd made a minor improvement to the pencil. It glowed in the dark and could be used as a personal fan with the push of a button.

"How's it going, G?" Li asked as they passed in the hallway.

"Better," Goldie replied.

And it was going better, until programming class. The teacher put all the students into teams of two. Goldie worried she might be partnered with Zeek, but she was set up with Ruby Rails. Goldie hadn't officially met Ruby yet, but she had heard about the stylish computer genius from Li.

"Hi! I guess we're partners," Goldie said, moving her chair next to Ruby. "I'm Goldie Blox."

"Nice to meet you." Ruby held up her minicomputer and snapped a picture. "So I can add you to my network."

"Okay." Goldie moved closer to the

classroom computer. "What are we supposed to be doing?"

"No worries, Goldie. I already finished the assignment." Ruby tapped the keyboard and the computer screen filled with strings of code.

"Um . . . great," Goldie said. But she didn't mean it. She wanted to work *with* Ruby.

"I'll explain it to you," Ruby said. "But I want you to answer my question first. Are you wearing the same thing you wore yesterday?"

"No," Goldie answered.

"Yes, you are. You wore overalls and a T-shirt yesterday," Ruby said.

"They aren't the *same* overalls and T-shirt. I have seven of each. One for each day of the week."

"That makes sense, I suppose." Ruby shrugged. "But I see fashion as a way to express yourself."

"Well . . . I guess I'm saying the same thing I said yesterday," Goldie said.

Ruby grinned. "You're funny."

The teacher gave them a warning look.

"Maybe we should get to work?" Goldie pointed at the computer.

Ruby slid over a sheet of paper with the assignment on it.

Create a program that scrambles a word that the user enters.

"I'll explain what I did. Writing code is my life," Ruby said. "Well, writing code *and* fashion are my life." She went over the basics with Goldie, and it made perfect sense. Ruby was a talented teacher.

Goldie tested the program. She typed in the word BUTTERFLY. Ruby's code spit out FUTLYBRET.

Their project was done, but there was still forty minutes left of class.

"What do we do now?" Goldie asked.

"I'm going to check in with my *Sew Good* network. It combines my two loves—"

"Coding and fashion," Goldie and Ruby said at the same time.

Ruby smiled. "I guess I just said that, huh?" Then she turned her attention to her sleek minicomputer.

"Do you mind if I play with this?" Goldie asked.

"Have a blast," Ruby replied without looking up.

Goldie entered more words.

SANDWICH came back WHACINDS.

TOOTHPASTE came back OPATTOHETS.

MY NAME IS GOLDIE came back with ERROR CODE 101.

Then Goldie had an idea. What if she tweaked the code so it could handle sentences?

She looked at Ruby, who was focused only on her minicomputer.

Goldie changed the second, fourth, and seventh line of Ruby's code. That didn't work. She played with line nine.

MY NAME IS GOLDIE came back with GNIEMOLMASEDYI.

"Yes!" she exclaimed.

The code worked fabulously, but Goldie knew it would be even more fun if it was less random. She hacked into Ruby's code again and linked it to an online dictionary. It took several tries, but with five minutes left in class, Goldie had done it.

MY NAME IS GOLDIE came back with I MEAN SMILEY DOG.

The teacher walked over to Ruby and Goldie's station. "Let's see your program," she said. "Knowing Ruby, I'm sure it's perfect."

"Yes, ma'am," said Ruby. She slipped her minicomputer into her custom handbag and reached for the keyboard.

"I got this," Goldie said.

Ruby sat back, allowing Goldie to demonstrate.

BUTTERFLY came back as FRY TUB LET.

"*Fry. Tub. Let.* Those are actually three words. Not exactly following the rules of the assignment." The teacher tapped her red pen against her grade book.

"That's not right," Ruby said. "I don't understand."

"It gets better." Goldie put her fingers on the keyboard. "Let's try another. *This is my favorite class.*"

THIS IS MY FAVORITE CLASS came back with SO I SAVE SLIM ITCHY FARTS.

"What does that say?" the teacher snarled.

Goldie quickly erased it. "How about this? *Higgs Bozon Prep is great.*" She typed.

"*Bizarre nights poop eggs?*" bellowed the teacher.

The entire class burst out laughing. Except Ruby. She shoved Goldie aside and took over at the computer. Ten seconds later the program was operating as she originally designed it.

Ruby showed it to the teacher.

FLOWER became WREFOL.

SMILE became LIEMS.

"Much, much better," the teacher said. Ruby breathed a sigh of relief. "Unfortunately, this came too late. Ruby and Goldie, you are getting a B on this assignment."

"Yes!" cheered Goldie. She held up her hand to give Ruby a high five. Ruby left her hanging.

"Why are you smiling?" Ruby asked. "That is *not* a good thing. I've never gotten a B. *Ever.*"

"Oh, sorry." Goldie pulled her hand back down. The bell rang.

"My life is ruined." Ruby stood up and chased the teacher. "I can't have a B. Let me do extra credit. Anything. Please."

Goldie sighed. Once again, she had messed up at HiBo Prep. She would have done *anything* to take back her code changes.

WOLVES DROWNING IN SYRUP

Goldie spotted Li waving to her from across the cafeteria. She was happy to see a friendly face. She carried her lunch tray over. Next to Li was a girl in a gray hoodie and pink glasses. She was the same girl who had given Goldie a click-o-matic pencil on her first day.

"Hey, G. Do you know Val?" Li asked as Goldie sat down.

"Sort of. We're both in Mr. Greg's class." Goldie gave Val her biggest smile. "I'm Goldie Blox, by the way."

Val took a bite of her sandwich.

Li opened a ketchup packet and tried to squeeze some on his burger but ended up shooting it into his hair.

Goldie laughed. "I never imagined you as a redhead."

"Ha-ha." Li tried to wipe it up with a napkin but made a bigger mess. "I'll be back." He left the two girls alone at the table.

Goldie munched on her pepperoni pizza. It was good but not very original. "At my old school, we used to have seaweed-and-pickle pizza every Thursday. And on the first Monday of the month, we had potato-chip-and-chicken-wing pizza. It was yummy. You just had to be careful of the bones." Goldie took another bite. "But this is tasty, too."

Val pulled her hood forward. Goldie could barely see her face.

"Hey, I never really thanked you for lending me a click-o-matic pencil. Well . . . I guess you didn't *lend* it to me, since I never gave it back. I owe you, Val." Goldie reached into her pockets and then her hair, looking for a way to repay Val. "Oh. Here." She held out half of a yo-yo. "I'm not sure where the other half is. I've checked my hair. It's not in here."

Val nibbled on her chips and didn't take the yo-yo. So Goldie slipped it into Val's open bag.

"We didn't have to use a certain kind of pencil at my old school," Goldie continued. "We could use any pencil or pen, or even spray paint. I think you would have liked it. I mean . . . what's not to like? We invented all kinds of cool stuff, like spray-paint erasers."

Goldie finished her pizza and slurped her chocolate milk.

Val sunk lower in her chair.

"You're really easy to talk to, Val," Goldie said. "Thanks for being so nice. It's been hard for me to make friends here. I don't always fit in with other kids."

Val broke her granola bar in half and gave Goldie the bigger piece.

"Thanks," Goldie said.

Li finally returned. His hair and shirt were wet. "It's hard to take a shower in a sink," he said.

"If I had a dozen straws, some tape, a funnel, and plastic wrap, I could've made you a shower," Goldie offered. Actually, she was carrying most of that stuff in her backpack—or in her hair.

Val's eyes grew wide in disbelief.

Goldie grinned. "I'm an inventor. A primo engineer. What do you like to do?"

When Val didn't answer, Li did for her. "Val and I are starting a band. She can play any instrument."

"Any instrument?" Goldie raised an eyebrow. Then she reached deep into her backpack and pulled out a gizmo that looked like a saxophone with a keypad welded to it and a plunger on the end.

"What is that?" Li asked.

"I haven't named it yet," Goldie said. "We can call it Awesome Instrument for now. It can imitate the sound of animals from birds to elephants."

She flipped an ON switch. The keypad lit up. Goldie lightly pressed the 9 button and put her mouth on the end.

Meow. It sounded like a tiny kitten had

joined them at their lunch table.

Val smiled.

"Wanna try it?" Goldie asked.

Val nodded. Goldie tapped a few keys, adjusted the plunger, and then handed it over.

"You're going to love this. I set it to jungle safari," Goldie said. "But watch out. If you're not careful, all the animal sounds will come out at once."

Li fidgeted. "Maybe this isn't a good—" But before he could finish his sentence, Val brought the instrument up to her mouth and blew.

The entire cafeteria filled with an awful noise. It didn't sound like an animal—well, maybe a pack of wolves drowning in syrup. Somehow the instrument was tied to the intercom. Val was playing for the whole school!

Val dropped the instrument, but it kept making awful noises.

"Val, make it stop!" someone yelled.

"Cut it out, Val!"

"Val Voltz is breaking my eardrums."

Goldie jumped up from her seat and grabbed the Awesome Instrument. She couldn't turn it off. So she threw it to the floor and stomped on it. Finally, it was silent.

"Whoopsie. Still some bugs to work out." Goldie laughed nervously.

Val's face was bright red under her hood.

"Thanks, new girl," a boy at the next table said to Goldie. "Val, that was the worst sound I've ever heard."

"It wasn't my . . . I didn't . . ." Val's voice broke as the whole cafeteria stared at her. She grabbed the edge of her hood and pulled it over her face.

"Val, I'm sorry," Goldie said. She wanted to say more, but Val got up and ran out.

Li chased after her.

Goldie dropped her head. That was it. She didn't belong at HiBo. She'd do anything to reopen the Blox School.

Anything.

A THREE-STEP PLAN

That evening, Goldie sat at her computer. She needed to reopen the Blox School. And she needed a team to help.

"I know at least three people who would like to see me gone from Higgs Bozon Prep." Goldie pressed SEND on her email to Val, Ruby, and Zeek.

SUBJECT: GET GOLDIE BLOX OUT OF HIGGS BOZON

Meet me in the BloxShop in an hour. We are going to reopen the Blox School. Can you make it?

All three replied immediately with YES!

Goldie got busy setting up for her meeting. She put out chairs and bowls of hot-sauce popcorn and chocolate-covered olives. Then she wrote down her plan on the whiteboard. She flipped it over so it could be unveiled at the right moment.

The BloxShop's doorbell gonged exactly one hour after she sent the message.

Goldie opened the door. "Hi, guys. Come on in."

"What is this place?" Zeek said, stepping inside. His Butler Phone hovered behind him.

"It's where I experiment and invent," Goldie said proudly.

"Looks like a junkyard." Ruby grimaced.

"Thanks." Goldie smiled. "Have a seat."

As Zeek, Ruby, and Val sank into their chairs, the door opened again. It was Li.

"Hey," he said to Goldie. "I came over to

see if you wanted to hang out." He poked his head through the door. "Are you having a party without me?"

"It's not a party," Zeek said.

"Goldie wants us to help her reopen her school," Ruby said.

"Her Goldie-proof school," Val added.

Li frowned. "What's wrong with Higgs Bozon?"

"Nothing," Goldie said. "I just miss my old school."

"Can we get started?" Zeek whined.

"Absolutely." Goldie turned over the whiteboard and proudly showed off her plan.

1. Form a team.

2. Rebuild the Blox School.

3. Leave Higgs Bozon.

"I guess I can cross off step one." Goldie grabbed a marker. "Wait. Before we rebuild the Blox School, we need a team name. Hmmm . . . What about Goldie and the Gearheads?"

"I'm not a Gearhead!" Zeek snapped.

"And that's not much of a plan," Val added.

"What happened to your old school?" Ruby asked.

"After I sent the second floor into outer space, the mayor closed it," Goldie explained.

"My dad is the mayor. I'll get him to reopen it," Zeek said. He spoke to his Butler Phone. "Call my dad and tell him—"

"Hang on," Li said. "The school is going to need some renovations before it can reopen."

"Exactly," Goldie said. "Step two."

Li grabbed the marker from Goldie. "We need to add a climbing wall. That'll make the Blox School epic!"

"I love it," Goldie said. "You know what else it needs?"

"A roof?" Val asked.

"An anti-gravity room. We can simulate life on the moon or on Mars." Goldie added her idea to the whiteboard.

"Why stop there?" Ruby snatched the marker. "You need a primo computer lab and a clean room."

"What's a clean room?" Goldie asked.

"Is that like a shower stall?" Li asked.

"No," Ruby answered. "A clean room has no dust or dirt. It has high-tech air filters. It's the perfect place to work on circuits. And . . . I just prefer a clean room to, you know, a normal room." She wiped some sawdust off the back of her chair.

"Sounds good," Goldie said. "Anything else?"

"Maybe a place for playing music," Val

suggested. Ruby added it to the list.

"What about you, Zeek?" Goldie asked.

"You're making this too complicated. All you need is four walls, a roof, and a door." Zeek

drew a square on the whiteboard. "Done."

"Okay," Ruby said. "Now we need blueprints, permits, materials,

and workers."

"Don't worry." Goldie tapped her head. "Everything we need is up here."

"Are you pointing to your brain or your hair?" Ruby asked.

Goldie pulled a tape measure from her blond curls. "Both! We start on Saturday. At eight a.m. sharp."

DUMPSTER DIVING

"Morning, Gearheads." Goldie and Nacho hopped off the deluxe skateboard they were sharing. Val, Ruby, and Zeek sat on the front step of the Blox School.

"Not a Gearhead," Zeek said.

"Did you bring blueprints?" Val asked.

"Nope."

"Did you bring a building permit?" Val started pacing.

"Nope."

"Materials?" Val looked like she might pass

out. *Is* no one *prepared?* she thought.

"That's a super place to start. We need materials to rebuild the school," Goldie said.

"Let's break into teams," Ruby suggested. "We'll get more done that way." She tapped away on her minicomputer. Ruby's purple hard hat matched her vest perfectly.

"That's a good idea," Goldie said. "You look nice, by the way."

"Thanks. We should be a team," Ruby said. "And if you're ever interested in a makeover, just let me know."

"I'm good with my overalls." Goldie stepped over next to Ruby. "But I'd love to be a team. Who wants to join us?"

Li arrived on his hoverboard. For someone with a million clocks in his house, he always managed to be late.

"Li and I will be our own team," Zeek said.

"Li, me, and Butler Phone."

"I'm honored, Master Zeek," the Butler Phone replied.

"That leaves you, Val," Goldie said. "Which team do you want to join?"

Val looked at the boys and then at the girls. She pulled her hood up and pointed at Nacho. "I pick the dog."

Nacho stopped licking his butt and smiled.

"Nacho can be a big help," Goldie said. "Sometimes."

"I was going to take some measurements for the roof." Val patted Nacho. "I'm sure the dog will come in handy."

The crew made a plan to gather supplies and meet back at the site in a few hours.

"Thanks, Gearheads. This is going to be fan-blastic." Goldie tried to get the teams to put their hands together in a huddle. Only Nacho was interested in a pre-building cheer.

The Butler Phone, Li, and Zeek took off right away.

"So," Ruby said. "Where should we go for supplies? The mall or one of those big hardware stores? Please say the mall. Please say the mall!"

"Nope." Goldie smiled. "I know the perfect spot. It's way cheaper than any store."

Ten minutes later, Goldie dove into a dumpster behind a construction site.

"That's disgusting," Ruby said.

"No, it's not." Goldie's head popped up out of the debris. "It's creative recycling. It's not like there's moldy cheese or dirty underwear in here. Come on."

Goldie began tossing stuff into a pile: wood, broken tiles, pieces of carpet, half a box of nails, and more.

"Are you sure there's nothing gross in there?" Ruby asked. She peered over the edge.

"It's all good," Goldie said as she flung out a length of rope.

Ruby put one foot over the dumpster wall and then the other. "I can't believe I'm doing this! I hope no one sees me." Her feet landed on a pile of cardboard.

"Look at all this cool stuff they were just going to throw out," Goldie said, grabbing some bricks.

"So what do we need?" Ruby asked. "And why didn't you tell me to bring gloves?"

"Anything. Everything. Whatever you think we can use."

In no time, the girls had dug through the entire dumpster. Their pile of stuff was taller than both of them combined. Then Goldie noticed something in the corner.

"Hey, grab that cable," she said to Ruby. "I bet we can use it for something."

"Sure." Ruby bent over and wrapped her fingers around the black cord. But it wasn't a cord.

Sssssss!

It was a snake! It hissed at Ruby, showing its pointy fangs.

"*Ahhhhh!*" Ruby screamed and threw the snake at Goldie.

"*Ahhhhh!*" screamed Goldie. She usually liked snakes and critters, just not when they were being thrown at her head.

Goldie stumbled back in the dumpster as the snake flew over her left ear. Her feet tangled in an old carpet. Cardboard and wood went flying. She landed headfirst in a cracked toilet tank.

"I'm stuck!" she shouted.

Ruby went from pinched and angry to amused. Her giggling echoed through the dumpster.

Goldie couldn't help it. She laughed, too.

"I hope that toilet's not used," Ruby gasped, wiping tears from her eyes.

"I hope that snake's not still in here," Goldie said.

That got Ruby's attention. She pulled Goldie from the toilet, and they were out of the dumpster in two seconds.

The girls filled wheelbarrows with their loot and walked back to the school. It was time to rebuild.

But when they returned, Li and Zeek had already started. Sort of.

"What is that?" Goldie pointed to a giant machine that was part crane, part robot.

"It's a BuildBot," Zeek explained. "I ordered it from Cube Co. We'll have this school rebuilt in no time, and then you'll be out of my life forever."

The BuildBot had already completed the second level. Everything was gray, sleek, and square.

"Bot, take five," Goldie said. "We'll handle it from here." She pulled on her safety goggles, and Nacho carried over a toolbox. They got to work.

Sawing.

Drilling.

Nailing.

Building.

Not surprisingly, they did very little measuring. Except Val. She placed every roof tile perfectly.

They continued through the day and the next day. Finally, the Blox School was complete. It wasn't huge, just five classrooms (including Val's music room and Ruby's clean room that had nothing in it), a cafeteria, bathrooms, and an epic climbing tower. There was plenty of space for learning and creating. From the outside, it looked like the result of a

hundred different architects. It was really the work of five.

"This is legendary," Li said.

"Totally," Goldie agreed.

Everyone loved the new school, except Zeek. "How soon before you're gone?"

"Soon," Goldie said. "But we need to do something else first."

AUTOMATIC ENVELOPE LICKER

The building was ready, but the Blox School needed funds to keep it open and for any future repairs. Goldie had the perfect idea for raising money—a gadget sale. It would be like a yard sale, but instead of broken lamps and chipped dishes, they would be selling awesome inventions.

The morning of the sale, Goldie put up tables in her front yard and covered them with old sheets. She set out some of her favorite creations. An automatic envelope licker.

A doggy backpack with a built-in pooper scooper. A ketchup-and-mustard gun. And a fork that changed into a spoon with the click of a button.

Val arrived first. She carried a dozen flutes, a beat-up saxophone, and three clarinets, and pushed a miniature grand piano.

"I don't have anything for the gadget sale," Val said. "But these are some old instruments."

Goldie's eyes lit up. "You don't have any gadgets *yet*!" She dragged Val and the instruments into her BloxShop. Then she tossed Val a pair of safety goggles before firing up the blowtorch.

Val watched in amazement as Goldie tore apart the instruments and then put them back together in a Frankenstein creation.

Goldie offered the first one to Val.

"No way," Val said. "It's probably some

crazy dog whistle that will start a stampede of rhinos."

"I wish. But no." Goldie blew into the instrument. The shop filled with a melody. The instrument looked like a flute but sounded like a grand piano—an off-key piano.

"You need to cut off exactly a half inch from the end," Val said. "And then it will be in tune."

Goldie followed Val's instruction, and the horn was perfect. Together, they created a bunch of them.

"You should keep one for the Blox School," Val suggested. "For music classes."

"That's a great idea!"

When they went back outside, Ruby was busy setting up her booth APPS BY RUBY RAILS.

She'd designed two new apps just for this occasion. One app selected the perfect nail polish color based on the user's favorite ice cream flavor. The other app was a master schedule for busy students. It helped fit in everything from homework to clubs and sports to favorite TV shows.

Ruby demonstrated. "I can do everything I want to do if I only sleep for thirty-seven minutes a night," she said proudly.

"That's thirty-six minutes longer than I thought you slept." Goldie shook her head.

Val set out the instruments while Goldie tried to put prices on everything.

"I can't decide between ten dollars and two thousand dollars," Goldie said, holding up the ketchup-and-mustard gun.

"If only there were numbers between ten and two thousand," Val joked.

Li wasn't selling gadgets. Instead, he had created a one-of-a-kind obstacle course for skateboarders in his front yard. It looped. It zigged. It zagged. It had a fifty-foot drop at the end.

"I wanted to have a moat with alligators," he said. "But the zoo said alligators were not available for sale or loan."

"Is that safe?" Val asked.

"I calculated everything perfectly," Li said. "Though you should still wear a helmet and knee pads."

"I wouldn't do that obstacle course if I was in a tank," Val said.

Nacho worked the cash box. If anyone tried to steal, they'd get slobbered on.

Zeek was the last to arrive. He set up his station with the touch of a button. The small briefcase he carried transformed into a shiny storefront.

"What are you selling, Zeek?" Goldie asked.

"Math homework," he answered proudly. "I'll do any math homework for one hundred dollars a page. Anything from kindergarten to college." Zeek laid out three super-complicated calculators.

"That's a lot of money," Ruby said.

"I guarantee A-plus work." He pointed to a sign that said just that.

"Hey, look. Our first customer," Li said.

A car pulled over on the side of the road, and a family of four got out. The boy and the girl rushed over to Li's obstacle course.

"How much? How much?" the girl asked.

"You can experience this physics-phenom for only fifty cents," Li said with a smile.

The boy reached into his pocket, but his mom grabbed his arm.

"I don't think so. Looks too dangerous," she said.

"Thank you," Li said, taking it as a compliment.

The mom guided her kids over to Ruby's booth.

"You'll never wonder what nail polish to wear ever again," Ruby explained.

"No, thank you." The mom joined the dad in front of Val's instruments. The little girl picked up an instrument. But instead of blowing into it, she banged it like a drumstick.

The dad yanked it away and said, "Sorry."

They weren't interested in Zeek's math homework for hire either. If the Gearheads were going to have their first sale, it would be up to Goldie.

"Perhaps a doggy backpack is what you're looking for?" Goldie suggested, and picked

up her pooper-scooper invention.

"We don't have a dog," the dad said.

"Can we have that dog?" the boy asked, pointing at Nacho.

"No," Goldie and the mom both answered.

"An automatic envelope licker?" Goldie held it up.

"Do you have any old lamps?" the dad asked. "I collect old lamps."

"Sorry, this isn't a yard sale," Goldie explained. "It's a gadget sale." She watched the first potential customers walk away.

Avocado-Chocolate-Bacon Smoothies

"It's early, Gearheads," Goldie said. "Don't lose hope. Here comes someone else, and we're not going to let her get away."

A woman in an oversized hat and a purple dress walked up the road. Everyone started talking to her at the same time.

"Slow down. Slow down," she said with a smile. "Maybe you can help me. I'm looking to buy blenders."

"Blenders and old lamps. That's all anyone wants." Val threw her hands in the air.

"My name is Miss Maggie," the woman continued. "And I'm opening Bloxtown's first smoothie shop, Frothy Formulas."

"I love smoothies!" Goldie yelled. "Will you have avocado-chocolate-bacon smoothies? But I don't like my smoothies with sesame seeds. That would be gross."

"I'll be able to make any kind of smoothie you like." Miss Maggie winked at Goldie. "With or without sesame seeds."

"Where is your shop?" Ruby asked.

"I don't have a place yet. I'm certainly on the lookout. But most of the locations I've seen are too expensive." Miss Maggie shook her head sadly.

"No duh," Zeek sneered. "Have you done any of the math, lady? If you calculate the cost of a store in Bloxtown and the cost of avocados, chocolate, bacon, and other supplies, you'd have to charge about twenty dollars a drink."

"That can't be true," Goldie said.

Zeek stared hard at Goldie. "Never doubt my math."

"I don't doubt your math skills," Goldie said. "But I doubt your being-nice skills."

Miss Maggie sighed. "I know it seems impossible, but I'm not going to give up. I'll find a way." She said goodbye and turned around.

The gadget sale's only customer walked back down the street.

"We're off to a slow start," Goldie said.

"It's not even a start. We're off to a stop," Val said.

"I knew this was a bad idea," Zeek said. "You're full of bad ideas, Goldie." He started packing away his calculators.

Goldie's heart sank. Zeek couldn't be right. "We can't give up," she said.

"I'm not giving up," Ruby said. She whipped out her minicomputer and pointed the tiny camera at Val. "Play the flute thingy."

And Val did. The yard filled with a jazzy piano sound that made everyone dance— except Zeek. He only tapped his toe.

"Fab! Now, Li, show off your obstacle course." Ruby pointed the camera in his direction.

Li jumped on a skateboard and zoomed through the course he'd designed. He rode it perfectly. He got some serious air on the final jump and sailed over their heads before landing softly.

"That was a ten!" Goldie yelled, holding up all her fingers.

"They should call you Gravity," Ruby said.

"Or Anti-Gravity," Val added.

"I like it. Li Gravity." Li gave them all a thumbs-up.

Ruby recorded a video of Zeek doing mind-blowing math problems. And he never even used one of his fancy calculators.

At last, Ruby filmed Goldie and her inventions. Goldie demonstrated each. Nacho even helped out on cue, pooping while wearing the backpack. The pooper scooper took care of the pile in a flash.

"Now what are you going to do?" Goldie asked when they were done.

"Give me a minute." Ruby tapped away on the minicomputer. They all watched, waiting for something big to happen. "And. There. It. Goes." She looked up and smiled.

"Where did it go?" Goldie asked.

"To everyone on my network," Ruby said.

"You think that's going to help?" Zeek laughed. "This is never going to work."

"*Never* isn't in my vocabulary," Goldie said.

"Is *useless* in your vocabulary?" Zeek asked. "I bet not even two people watch the video. I bet—"

But before Zeek could finish his sentence, a bus pulled up. Then several cars and a trolley. The road was jammed.

"That's what I'm talking about!" Goldie gave Ruby a hug. They were in business.

SIXTY-SEVEN DECIBELS

The next week, Goldie walked down the halls of Higgs Bozon Prep with her head held high. They'd earned enough money at the gadget sale to reopen the Blox School.

"Hey, Zeek." She waved.

"You're still here?" he moaned.

"Hopefully not for much longer." Goldie and the Gearheads just needed permission from the mayor to open the school.

"The sooner, the better," Zeek said.

"The next step is up to you," she reminded

him. "We need a meeting with the mayor."

"My dad is a very busy man."

"Hey, Butler Phone," Goldie said. "Can you send an invitation to Mayor Zander? Dinner. Tomorrow night." Then she gave the address to the Blox School. "But don't mention my name or the Blox School. I want it to be a surprise." Goldie suspected the mayor wouldn't show up if he knew the reason for the dinner.

"Certainly, Miss Blox," the Butler Phone replied.

"Hey, you don't take orders from her," Zeek snapped.

"Sorry, Master Zeek," the phone said.

"I'm going to convince your dad to open the school. Will you help me?" Goldie asked Zeek.

Zeek snorted. "Good luck. My dad never changes his mind. *Never*."

"Or I could just stay at Higgs Bozon."

Goldie smiled. "Maybe I could join your young geniuses club? Or your math team?"

"No!" Zeek said. "Butler Phone, send the invitation to my father. We need to get rid of Goldie."

"Thanks, Zeek." She patted him on the back and walked toward the cafeteria.

Li wasn't there. He had a meeting with the physics team. Goldie worried she might have to sit alone, but then Ruby and Val waved her over.

"Sit, Goldie," Ruby said. "We're working on our presentation for the mayor. Check this out." She tapped on her minicomputer and a hologram of the Blox School appeared over the table.

"Awesome!" Goldie touched the image with one finger, but of course, there was nothing there.

Val was writing in a notebook. She had pages and pages of text. Her taco lay untouched.

"What's that, Val?" Goldie asked.

"She's writing our speech," Ruby answered for her.

Goldie stared. "That has to be five thousand words. You've never said that many words in your life, Val."

"Never had to," Val said.

The girls laughed.

"You know what else we need?" Goldie said as she dug into her plate of spaghetti. "Special effects. Like a fog machine and a laser light show."

"How about you make a few posters," Val suggested.

"Talking posters," Goldie said. "Val, that's terrific!"

Goldie jotted down the idea in her notebook. Then she took a big drink of her chocolate milk. The spaghetti, the milk, and the excitement crashed in her stomach, and she let out a huge *BURP!* It made the entire cafeteria go quiet.

"Sorry." Goldie patted her chest. "It got away from me."

"That was gross," Ruby said, but she was laughing under her scowl.

"I've heard better," Val said, not looking up from her notes.

"No way!" Goldie said. She was always up for a challenge. Any challenge. She searched through her backpack and pulled out a device the size of a deck of cards.

"What is that?" Val asked.

"A sound meter," Goldie said. "Let's see who has the best burp."

"Don't you mean let's *hear*?" Val smiled. She opened her bottle of fizzy water and guzzled half of it.

Well, that's not fair, Goldie thought.

Val squeezed her eyes and mouth closed. She tilted her head. Goldie and Ruby watched. Seconds ticked off the clock. Val looked like she might explode.

"Val, are you okay?" Ruby whispered.

Then Val opened her mouth and burped. She aimed it right at the sound meter. The noise was impressive. She turned it around to show Goldie and Ruby the results.

Sixty-five decibels.

"Nice," Goldie said. "My turn."

She drank. She ate. She belched into the machine.

Sixty-seven decibels.

"Yes!" Goldie cheered. Her first had

probably been even louder, but still, she was the champion.

Or so she thought. Val pulled the sound meter out of her hands and gave it to Ruby.

"No way," Ruby said. "We're not in kindergarten."

"A kindergartner couldn't burp that loud," Goldie said.

"Chicken," Val said. That was all Ruby needed.

Without even taking a drink, Ruby held the sound meter to her mouth and *BUUUURRRRP*ed. Goldie and Val looked at each other, their ears ringing. They knew they'd been beaten.

Seventy-nine decibels.

"That has to be a world record," Goldie said.

"You think so?" Ruby looked it up on her

minicomputer. It wasn't a record. Not even close. The top burp was about one hundred and ten decibels. "People actually enter burping contests."

"You should do it," Goldie said. "With some practice, you could be a champion. I could help you train."

When lunch was over, they walked to gym class together, still giggling. And when the teacher told them to form three-person teams to play basketball, the girls didn't even need to ask each other. They were a team.

"Just don't call us Gearheads," Val said.

"Okay," Goldie said. But she secretly believed they'd come around to the name.

Ruby wasn't as good at basketball as she was at burping. But luckily, Goldie had brought an extra pair of her floaty sneakers. Val dribbled the ball up the court like a pro, and

Ruby and Goldie could slam-dunk, thanks to the sneakers.

They scored and scored ten more times, winning the game.

"That's not fair," Zeek complained. He was on the losing team. "It's because of those sneakers."

"There are no rules about sneakers," Ruby said as she high-fived Goldie.

Zeek called out to his Butler Phone.

"Order me a pair of those flying sneakers," he demanded.

"You can't buy them, Zeek," Goldie explained. "I invented them. I could make you a pair if you want."

Zeek stormed off the court. "I'm done. I have a cramp." His Butler Phone followed him, apologizing for not being able to order the sneakers.

"You guys should transfer to the Blox School," Goldie said. "We'd have so much fun."

"It would be fun, but Val and I belong at Higgs Bozon. You understand, right?" Ruby asked.

Goldie's heart sank. "Yeah, I understand."

AN ICE CREAM DINNER

The ice cream dinner at the new Blox School had been Val's idea. Three courses of ice cream, with milk shakes to drink. No way could the mayor be grumpy after all that ice cream. And they needed him to be in a good mood.

Goldie and Nacho rode a skateboard to the Blox School. Goldie had fitted a cooler with souped-up wheels and a motor to tow the ice cream. They brought seven flavors, including gooey dog biscuit. Goldie also packed a suitcase filled with emergency supplies.

"This is it, Nacho," Goldie said. "Tonight will change my future forever."

Nacho barked in agreement.

Val and Ruby arrived early to help set up. They'd never seen someone use an electric drill to mix milk shakes.

"That's genius," Ruby said.

Val and Ruby moved a table to the front

classroom. Goldie covered it with a shimmery cloth that changed colors with the temperature.

"Goldie, what's in there?" Val asked, pointing to the suitcase by the door.

"Please tell me it's nothing that will blast off," Ruby added.

"I promise. No rockets." Goldie didn't want to tell anyone what she *had* brought.

Li joined them. He rode his skateboard from room to room, making sure everything in the school was perfect.

Crash!

"I'm okay," Li yelled.

"Focus, people. Val, keep a lookout," Ruby ordered. "Is everything ready?" She used her minicomputer to review the details and check off each item.

"We're golden!" Goldie smiled.

"They're here," Val said a second later, and

Nacho barked.

They all huddled around the door. Goldie took a deep breath.

A large black SUV came to a stop next to the school. The back doors automatically opened. Zeek got out first, and then Mayor Zander. The mayor was frowning. He looked grumpy.

"We may need more ice cream," Goldie whispered.

Mayor Zander eyed the school like it was a trap. "What is this?" he yelled. Even from inside, they could hear him.

"It's the Blox School," Zeek said. "You closed it a few weeks ago because of a hole in the roof. But now it's fixed. It needs to be reopened."

"All this school needs is a few minutes with a wrecking ball," the mayor said. He turned around to get back in the car.

"Oh no! He's not coming in," Ruby said.

Li pushed open the door. "Your Majesty Mayor, sir. Wait. We have ice cream."

The mayor ignored Li. "Zeek, get in the car. We're leaving."

Ruby and Val ran outside, too.

"Stop." Val held up her hand.

"You can't go. We've worked so hard," Ruby begged.

The mayor ignored their pleas. Goldie knew what she had to do. She grabbed her suitcase and found what she needed. Less than a minute later, she had it set up in front of an open window.

She aimed.

She pulled the lever.

Boom!

The net cannon fired perfectly.

"Hey, it worked," she said to Nacho,

slightly amazed.

The net landed on the mayor.

"I'm trapped!" he screamed. He fought against the ropes but only got more tangled.

"Don't struggle!" Goldie yelled to him. But it was too late. The mayor was completely wrapped up. He tripped and fell to the ground.

NO ONE IS GOING TO JAIL

"**Y**ou killed the mayor!" Ruby screamed.

Goldie ran over to Mayor Zander.

"I'm not dead," he grumbled.

"See, he's breathing." Goldie gave Ruby two thumbs up.

"And talking," Val pointed out.

"Untangle me!" the mayor ordered.

Ruby pulled one way. Li pulled another. They weren't getting anywhere.

"Wait," Goldie said. "I've got scissors to cut you free. But first, I need you to listen to us."

"I don't want to be part of this." Zeek crossed his arms and closed his eyes, as if not watching made it all go away.

"Dude, you are already a part of this," Li said.

Ruby and Val helped the mayor sit up. He was still safely stuck in Goldie's net. Ruby leaned in and whispered to Goldie, "I think this is kidnapping."

"This is not kidnapping," Goldie said, not bothering to whisper. "He's not a kid, and he's not napping."

"It's more like mayor fishing," Val added.

Ruby pulled out her minicomputer and tapped on the keyboard. "Do you want to know the prison sentence for kidnapping?"

"I don't want to know," Val said.

Ruby answered anyway. "Eight years. We could go to jail for eight years."

"No one is going to jail." Goldie hoped she was right.

"Enough!" the mayor growled. "What do you kids want?"

"Hi, I guess we haven't really met yet. I'm Goldie Blox. And I need to talk to you about reopening this fine school. The Blox School two-point-oh." Goldie pointed her thumb at the school.

"I know who you are. And I know what you did to this school. The entire second story was destroyed." The mayor yanked on the net, trying to break free.

"But we rebuilt it, and it's better than ever," Goldie said.

"I'm not interested," the mayor said. "Zeek, get me out of here. Now!"

"Hey, Dad." Zeek stepped forward. "I need to say some things first. Like this wasn't my idea. None of it."

Goldie rolled her eyes.

"Zeek Zander, you do not—" began the mayor.

"Just listen," Zeek interrupted his dad. "We need another school in Bloxtown. Higgs Bozon Prep isn't for everyone."

Goldie pointed to herself to make sure the mayor understood.

"Higgs Bozon is a place of order and high achievement. We're number one in the country for math and science and locker cleanliness. Goldie messes that all up. She's a B student."

"B-plus," Goldie corrected him.

"And her locker is a disaster," Zeek said. "I think she's growing something in there."

"There may be some genetic engineering going on. I accidentally crossed a Venus flytrap with a cactus." Goldie shrugged. "I wouldn't open that locker if I were you."

"She's never prepared for class," Zeek continued. "Doesn't have the right supplies. Always loses stuff. It slows down the rest of the class. She ruins everything."

"Hey! That's not true," Ruby interrupted. "Goldie doesn't slow anything down. She keeps everyone, especially the teachers, on their toes. We did three extra experiments on gravity in Mr. Greg's class."

"And one of those experiments led to an egg landing on Mr. Greg's head," Zeek explained. "How do you expect to keep good teachers if they get hit in the head with eggs?"

Goldie laughed, remembering what her teacher looked like with egg on his bald head. Mr. Greg had not laughed, but his Teachatron 5000 had.

"Goldie has also changed the menu in the

cafeteria," Zeek said.

She'd only suggested they add a make-your-own-waffle bar. It had been a hit.

"She broke the basketball hoop."

She'd merely bent it.

"And those squirrels that invaded the music room. I bet they snuck in in her crazy hair."

"I've never had squirrels in my hair. Chipmunks . . . maybe." Goldie ran a hand through her curls. She was currently critter-free.

"Dad, this is just the start. What if she joins our clubs or runs for school president? She cannot represent Higgs Bozon Prep." Zeek was breathing hard, like he'd lost at basketball again. "But don't take it just from me." He looked at Ruby and Val. "They all agree."

Ruby fidgeted. "Well . . . she's not your

average HiBo student, but I kind of hope she stays."

"You do?" Goldie asked, surprised.

Ruby nodded. "This school is cool, too. I get it if you want to be a Blox School student. It's your choice. But I'd miss you. Things would be boring. Less messy, but boring."

Goldie laughed.

"One more thing, Mr. Mayor," Ruby said. "I had nothing to do with catching you in this net. And if you don't send us to jail, I'm sure my parents will vote for you in November."

"Every vote counts," Mayor Zander said. He smiled, but it looked fake.

Zeek stepped in front of Ruby and whispered, "That wasn't very helpful."

Ruby shrugged.

Zeek turned to Val and begged, "Say something. Tell my dad why Goldie needs to go. She embarrassed you."

"True," Val said. "But not on purpose."

"She never has a plan," Zeek continued.

"True." Val nodded.

"She talks too much," Zeek said.

"I know someone else who talks too much." Val raised her eyebrows.

"She's not like anyone else," Zeek said.

Val nodded again. "True."

"She needs to go to her own school. She doesn't belong at Higgs Bozon." Zeek smiled triumphantly.

"Not true," Val said.

Zeek's smile collapsed.

Val shrugged. "Life would be ordinary without Hurricane Goldie."

"That's the nicest thing you've ever said to me, Val." Goldie beamed.

"Li, buddy, help me out here." Zeek put his

arm around Li's shoulder.

Li shook his head. "You know, I've been Goldie's best friend and neighbor since before she got her first power tool."

"Never mind." Zeek pushed Li away. "Goldie, you tell him."

"I don't know what to say." Goldie hesitated. "I loved my old school. And I love this school we rebuilt together. But I also—"

"*Buuuuzzzz.*" Zeek cut her off. "Time's up."

"Yes. Time is up," Mayor Zander said. "I've made up my mind."

Goldie braced herself for what was coming next.

A PROUD HIGGS BOZON CUBE

Mayor Zander took a giant breath before he started yelling at Goldie and her crew. "I've never been treated with such disrespect!"

"Sorry. We just needed you to listen." Goldie tried to talk over his yelling. "We didn't really think that—"

"You didn't think at all!" Mayor Zander agreed. "That's the problem. You, Miss Goldie Blox, are trouble. You are a disgrace to this town and to Higgs Bozon Prep. I've never met an unrulier troublemaker in my life. You're a rotten apple, and I will not let you ruin the bushel."

"Enough of the name-calling," Ruby said.

"Dad." Zeek stepped forward. "Are you going to reopen the Blox School or not?"

The mayor glared at Goldie. "If reopening the school keeps you from tarnishing the reputation of Higgs Bozon Prep and interfering with the education of my son, then I will personally see it done."

Zeek broke out into an awkward dance. "Oh yeah! Here we go! Oh yeah!" he sang, and his Butler Phone provided a background beat. He even tried to do a cartwheel but accidentally kicked his dad in the nose. "Sorry about that," he said, still dancing.

"Just cut me free!" the mayor demanded.

Nacho fetched a pair of scissors. No one else danced or sang as Zeek freed his dad.

"Let's get out of here," Mayor Zander said.

"Right behind you." Zeek followed his dad to the SUV. Before they drove off, Zeek unrolled the window and yelled to Goldie, "It was *not* nice knowing you. And I hope to never see you again."

Li, Ruby, Val, and Goldie stood quietly.

"I guess we won," Goldie finally said with a shrug.

"I guess," Ruby said.

"Should we celebrate?" Goldie asked. She didn't feel like celebrating.

"Let's clean up," Ruby answered.

Goldie and her friends went into the school and packed up everything from the dinner party. Then they left. No one talked about what would happen next.

When Goldie got home, she was starving. She went to the kitchen and heated up a plate of mac and cheese. She sprinkled bacon bits and garbanzo beans on top.

Her mom walked into the kitchen with a

pile of papers and joined Goldie at the table.

"Lots of projects to grade," her mom said.

"Just put an A on every one of them. All the kids at HiBo get As," Goldie said.

"What's wrong?" her mom asked. "How did your big dinner meeting go?"

"Great. And not great." She pushed her mac and cheese around on her plate but didn't eat any.

"That sounds complicated," her mom said.

"I got what I wanted. The mayor agreed to reopen the Blox School." Goldie sighed.

"Oh," her mom said.

"But I'm not sure if I want to go back." Goldie sank lower in her chair. "I don't exactly fit in at Higgs Bozon. But I kind of like it. And

I definitely like Val, Ruby, and Li. They're my Gearheads."

"Gearheads?" her mom asked.

"Yeah, I named them. They're cool with it." Goldie wondered if they'd wear jackets with GEARHEADS written on them. She knew Ruby could design something pretty awesome.

Her mom gave her a hug. "Goldie, it's okay to change your mind."

"But what about you?" Goldie asked. "You don't like Higgs Bozon. Do you? You want to go back to teaching at the Blox School. Right?"

"Well . . ." Her mom played with a piece of hair hanging in her face. "To be honest, I like Higgs Bozon."

"You do?" Goldie asked.

"Yeah, I do. I get to teach lots of kids. We get all the best equipment. And today we started growing a new species of carnivorous plant in the classroom. They say it can grow as big as a

114

car!" Her mom smiled. "I'm doing what I love. It's pretty nice."

"Better than the Blox School?"

"Not better or worse," her mom said. "But I'd be happy to stay at HiBo. I don't exactly fit in either. But I'm making a difference."

Goldie nodded. "Yeah. That's the best way to make a difference, by not fitting in."

"Does that mean we're staying?" her mom asked.

Goldie gave her mom a big smile. "Yes, it does."

The next day at school, Zeek walked right into his Butler Phone when he saw Goldie in the hallway.

"You aren't supposed to be here!" he yelled.

"Sorry, Master Zeek," the Butler Phone answered.

"Not you. Her!" He pointed at Goldie.

"Change of plans, Zeek. I'm a proud Higgs Bozon Cube after all." Goldie pulled on her new Higgs Bozon hat.

"No. No. No!" Zeek stomped down the hallway.

Ruby and Val stepped out of a classroom.

"Is that true?" Ruby asked. "Are you staying?"

"Yep," Goldie said. "I realized that Higgs Bozon has a lot to offer."

"Like state-of-the-art technology?" Ruby asked.

"That's not what I was talking about," Goldie said. "I'm more interested in the Gearheads."

"If you're staying, the school should probably get more insurance," Val added.

Li joined them. He already knew Goldie was sticking around since they rode their skateboards to school together. "I just passed Zeek. He looked like he saw a ghost." Li laughed.

"Well, I'm glad you're staying, Goldie," Ruby said. "But what's going to happen to the Blox School? We did a really fabulous job rebuilding it."

"Don't worry. I have an idea," Goldie said.

"An idea?" Val said. "Should I put on a hard hat and goggles?"

NEVER!

Goldie's plan did not require hard hats or safety goggles. All she needed was the building permit she had gotten from Mayor Zander and a hammer to hang a new sign on the old Blox School.

FROTHY FORMULAS SMOOTHIE SHOP

AND COMMUNITY CENTER

Miss Maggie had loved the idea of opening her smoothie shop in the old school. She might not have imagined a store with a climbing wall, a clean room, and a net cannon.

That was all bonus.

Goldie and her friends were special guests for the grand opening. Goldie even helped Miss Maggie cut the ribbon with a giant pair of scissors.

"Three . . . two . . . one . . . ," Miss Maggie counted down. "Frothy Formulas is now officially open!"

Goldie joined her friends in line to get a

smoothie. She practically fell over when she saw Ruby take off her long jacket.

"Overalls!" Goldie shrieked. "You look incredible, Rubes."

"Thanks," Ruby said. "Don't get too excited. I'm not going to wear them every day. But I'll admit, I love all the pockets. This pouch can even fit my minicomputer."

When they got to the counter, they each ordered a large smoothie, and Miss Maggie wouldn't accept their money. Li got a chocolate-banana smoothie with protein powder. Ruby had a berry bonanza. Val, who took the longest to order, got a coffee blast. Then it was Goldie's turn.

"I want an everything smoothie," she said. "But hold the sesame seeds."

"That sounds disgusting," Ruby said.

"Sounds like Goldie," Li said.

"And two vanilla smoothies," Goldie continued ordering.

When the drinks were ready, Goldie grabbed the two vanilla smoothies and told her friends she'd be right back.

They watched as she walked across the street. Zeek and Mayor Zander stood on the curb, keeping their distance from Frothy Formulas.

"Here." Goldie shoved the vanilla smoothies into their hands.

Mayor Zander grumbled, but Zeek took a big gulp.

"It was nice of you to come," Goldie said. "And you're just in time."

"For what?" Zeek asked.

Goldie pulled a remote control from her pocket. Then she pressed the big red button in the center. A disco ball popped out of the roof.

Flickering lights danced across the crowd, and everyone oohed and aahed.

"You were supposed to leave Higgs Bozon," Zeek snarled. "That was the deal."

Goldie shrugged. "I changed my mind. I like it there."

"Dad, can't we kick her out?" Zeek asked.

"No," Mayor Zander said. "I had my lawyers look into it. If she chooses to attend Higgs Bozon Prep, there's nothing I can do about it." He still hadn't taken a single sip of his smoothie.

"You'll never fit in at HiBo, Goldie Blox." Zeek leaned forward so his face was only a few inches from hers.

"I don't want to fit in," she said. "I want to blow the roof off the place."

The Zanders' mouths fell open.

"Just kidding." Goldie smiled. "But a rocket

launch is not totally out of the question. Especially since I was just voted captain of the new Space Exploration Club. Zeek, you're welcome to join."

"Never!" Zeek stuck his chin in the air.

"Never? Hmmm. That word isn't in my vocabulary." Goldie grinned and walked back to her friends. She couldn't wait for new adventures to come their way.